Stand Corrected

Issue #14

**Spanking erotica for
the 21st century
from Shadow Lane**

www.shadowlane.com

CCB Publishing, British Columbia, Canada

Stand Corrected Issue #14

Spanking erotica for the 21st century
from Shadow Lane

Editor **Eve Howard**

Contributing Designer **Butch Simms**

Contributing editor **Zille Defeu**

Photography by **Butch Simms**, **Tony Elka**
and **Evil Malc**

Illustrations by **Brian Tarsis**

visit us at **www.shadowlane.com**

Follow Eve Howard on Twitter **@EveShadowLane**

Follow Tony Elka on Twitter **@Tony_ShadowLane**

On Fetlife.com follow: **EveHoward** and
Shadow Lane Labor Day 2015
for the latest updates

Stand Corrected Issue #14:
Spanking Erotica for the 21st Century
from Shadow Lane

Copyright ©2015 by Shadow Lane
ISBN-13   978-1-77143-237-5
First Edition

Library and Archives Canada Cataloguing in Publication
Howard, Eve, 1953-, editor
Stand corrected issue #14 : spanking erotica for
the 21st century from Shadow Lane
/ edited by Eve Howard. -- First edition.
Issued in print and electronic formats.
ISBN 978-1-77143-237-5 (pbk.).--
ISBN 978-1-77143-238-2 (pdf)
Additional cataloguing data available from
Library and Archives Canada

The romance of discipline, spanking photography, spanking fiction,
spanking advice, spanking roleplay, domestic discipline, spanking
video erotica, spanking editorials, corporal punishment pictorials.

Publisher: CCB Publishing
          British Columbia, Canada
          www.ccbpublishing.com

Zille Defeu featured at left
and on previous page

Stand Corrected

magazine returns in time for the troubled teens of the 21st century, an era of exponentially expanded opportunity for spanking enthusiasts. The internet and social media are getting people out of their shells every minute of every day in just about every corner of the world. And as regards our scene, these modern communication techniques are making it possible for more of us to meet and play, adventure, fall in love, and even enjoy classic happily-ever-after endings. Granted, there are dangers one needs to be aware of, just as there are when frequenting actual cruising bars. Common sense and good instincts are key to conducting successful online courtships and seductions, finding the best parties and obtaining the most reliable referrals. But think of the two powerhouse tools now at all of our command as we contemplate the vast scene pool: limitless space for the printed word and the ability to post color images. We can currently attract someone's attention at dizzying speed, which opens up even more possibilities for hooking up during travel and vacations, not to mention coordinating rendezvous at spanking parties.

I first came out in the 1980's, when magazines with personal ads formed the network that held the scene together. These days spanking people of all ages reach out to each other through websites, blogs and Fetlife™. And yet even with all of this exposure, it still takes a certain type of (alpha-spanking?) personality to be proactive enough to meet for a play date or go to a party.

For those of us who have been compelled to take it to the next level, the desire to engage has been too insistent to indefinitely ignore. Even if we were paranoid (about someone finding out) or afraid (of being victimized by a creep or scammer) or even insecure about our looks or age or prospects, we had to eventually follow through and have our first encounter with another human being in the scene.

My favorite part of our recent spanking survey was the question, "How did your first real play date go?" The response was overwhelmingly positive. This didn't surprise me. We spanking people don't need that much to make us happy once we find each other.

This reboot of our classic magazine Stand Corrected, includes a scrapbook of my favorite pix from some of my recent spanking videos. I've gotten a lot of feedback from spanking enthusiasts who have been following me since my early Nu-West days and most of them approve of my going dom. A few cranky tops have crabbed about it, reminding me of articles I wrote a quarter century ago about *never* wanting to spank others. This sentiment is echoed by a lot of subbed-out girls. But as Aldous Huxley observed, "The only completely consistent people are dead." (That man knew everything, and he also stuck neat spanking references into his books and stories.)

Enjoy the new Stand Corrected and please email your comments to:
Eve@shadowlane.com

Stand Corrected

Issue #14

Table of Contents

page 24

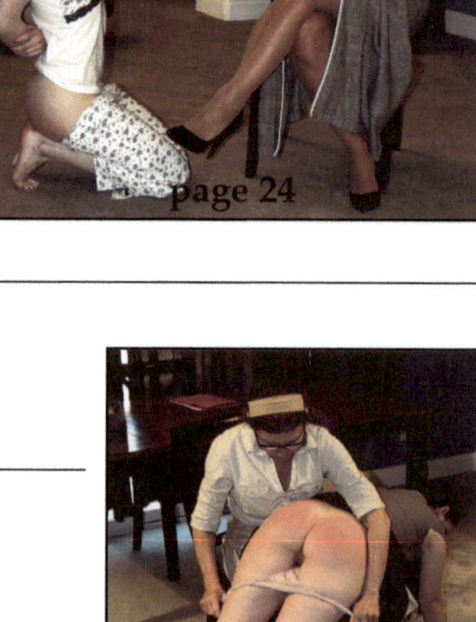

page 48

page 61

page 63

What is Shadow Lane?
Shadow Lane is a company that has been celebrating the
Romance of Discipline, through books, publications, videos,
social media, personal ads and gala parties, since 1986. The
first spanking producer that began to consider what a female
spanking enthusiast might want in her erotica, Shadow Lane
remains the preferred studio for romantic and erotic boy
spanks girl entertainment. Sadly, all of our early Stand Corrected
magazines are out of print, but all Shadow Lane fans will want to
add our elegant Art of Spanking magazine to their secret collection.
Order **Shadow Lane's The Art of Spanking**, in print from:
shadowlane.com, or from amazon.com or CCBPublishing.com
for $19.95 or e-zine format from amazon.com and other e-book
retailers for $9.95

Zille Defeu
Interview with a retro minx who
loves that her husband spanks her

Eve: The first time I saw you at a party, I was slain by your retro look. How much of a retro girl are you in real life?

Zille: I'm a strange mix of retro and futuristic! Actually, the main "retro" which I am is Victorian. My favourite porn is Victorian erotica, and I love wearing corsets and bloomers!

The fifties comes in for me in two ways. One, it's the time period closest to our own that I can look to for a role model of how to work a relationship being the submissive that I am. And, also, the fifties were the last time that women had all the elegance that comes of having all those proper details of dressing: foundation garments, stockings, gloves, hats – that sort of thing. Our modern life does not have enough of those to suit me!

On the other hand, I don't really want to live without digital photography or the internet … so I try and fulfil my retro fantasies while enjoying the perks of this modern life!

Eve: Are you a bossy girl in real life and if so, how do you make that work within the context of a relationship where you are the sub?

Zille: Well, if I'm in a situation where I need to be in charge, I can do it, and do it well. But mostly I prefer to be submissive, and take orders rather than give them. Or, politely make suggestions, rather than give orders. I like who I am much better when I am making myself work to be polite and finding ways to work around just saying, "No, I don't want to do that," or "I think that's a bad idea – *my* idea is better!" It turns out you can do all those things in a well-mannered and respectful way. I really do find that far more rewarding, and I think it makes me a better, stronger person.

Eve: You're a notorious anglophile. How did you acquire your English husband and how much of the attraction was due to his being a Brit? Which begs the question, how do you feel about caning?

Zille: I was introduced to Mr. Defeu at a party, by a kinky friend, who said to him, "Here's a model who makes kinky porn – work with her!" and turned to me and said, "Here's a friend who shoots kinky photographs – work with him!" But at that time, I was with a long-term partner, and even though we were poly, she sensed how attracted to him I was at first sight, and put him out of bounds! (He was the *only* person she ever did that with!)

So Mr. Defeu shot me with her on several occasions. And did some solo shoots with me as well, as time went by. I was always terribly excited to work with him – but I couldn't go any further than flirt with him from in front of the camera!

Finally, I was available at the same time that he was available! He actually spanked me *before* our first official date, and we started being Dom and sub on that first date! The rest is history!

As for the cane, I've written about it before, so I hope you don't mind me quoting that:

> A caning hurts. *Quite a lot.* It's a white-hot slash of pure pain that shocks you upon impact … and then builds up and up until you think you may go crazy. And then, when it's died down to the point when you are thinking that *maybe* sanity is an option again … the next stroke comes slashing down…!
>
> *And it's the hottest, hottest thing in the whole wide world.*

The rest of what I wrote is here: http://www.zilledefeu.com/spank/the-cane-what-you-really-think/

Eve: How high up does spanking and domestic discipline rank within your BDSM interests?

Zille: It's the complete and utter top of the list. I was really only doing all that BDSM stuff because I found the BDSM scene before I found the spanking scene. Mr. Defeu introduced me to the spanking scene, and I immediately switched allegiance!

Not that I couldn't still manage to have fun in a dungeon. And I'm still fond of tentacle monster anime porn! But I'd always rather be off in the headmaster's office!

A graceful and elegant retro girl, Zille expresses the spirit of the 1950's by donning dainty, full coverage foundation garments for many of her photo shoots. Open bottomed girdles and seamed hose are essential accessories when recreating a vintage look.

As for domestic discipline, for me that's just part and parcel of spanking. I'd rather be in a dom/sub situation. And I am really into real life punishments. (Well – except when I'm right in the middle of receiving one – at which point you'd get a very different story from me!) I wish it was easier to work those things into day-to-day life!

Eve: How old were you when you first got a boy or man to spank you?

Zille: I knew I was into spanking when I started reading Robert Heinlein when I was 17. I don't know why I didn't get my then-boyfriend to spank me, because we were playing around with bondage and roleplay anyway!

It was in college that I first asked a boy to spank me. He did so, but besides really enjoying leaving a red handprint, it did nothing for him – and so it didn't do much for me, either!

After that followed a long period where I was really confused because I knew for certain I was kinky, but I didn't think I was really a masochist. So I explored all the myriad avenues of BDSM and fetish. And I had some fun while I was at it, but nothing really 100% met my needs.

Getting together with Mr. Defeu changed all that for me!

Eve: You've done some pretty extreme videos. What's the appeal been for you in testing your limits?

Zille: Well, I've seen Lupus films, and I honestly don't think I've done anything that extreme – at least pain-wise! I've made some weird (and for me quite fascinating) porn over the years, but that just challenged me to make good porn that satisfied customers – which is something which really makes me feel good about myself.

I guess all the spanking porn I've made is really more about testing my limits in the whole: acting well – and keeping it up under duress! – and also remembering to keep a good angle to the camera – and at the same time making sure the whole thing is authentic and HOT – that's the limit I really am pushing.

During shooting, pain can and will still hurt as much as usual. But I'm so focused on the ends, that I can get through the means! Indeed, I

continued on page 11

A domestic goddess naturally possesses a complete wardrobe of attractive aprons, which are sometimes actually worn over a dress.

think I may have a higher (or longer, really) pain tolerance when I am on a set. Because I have other things to think about at the time! When I'm at home doing a scene with Mr. Defeu, then all I have to think about is the pain, and so I might be brought to tears a good deal faster!

Eve: You're a highly enthusiast top, please explain how this fits into your scene persona.

Zille: Well, it all fits in if you know that what I am is a "service top"! That is, I want to give any person who is subbing to me the most perfect, fulfilling experience I can. The scene is totally about them … in the end, I really still am being submissive to their wants and needs.

I *can* enjoy being a bit of a sadist. Some wild mischief can come alive in me in those moments! But in the end, I really just want to be the one being spanked!

Eve: What is it you like about wearing vintage corsetry? Is it that it affords the most protection against a paddle or strap? It is certainly not convenient to wear. Is that part of the charm?

Zille: Corsets and girdles and things like that are a bit like bondage: they are very restrictive, and hold you in a tight, comforting embrace. I like the constriction and restriction! And the fact that they are all finicky things that add to the care it takes in dressing, and only being able to move in certain (often more graceful ways) just add to my pleasure in wearing them.

I don't want or need protection – well, unless you *do* mention that paddle! I *hate* paddles, and you could not stuff my knickers with enough McGuffy's Readers when a paddle is threatened! But seriously, I'm not really into getting bent over and then not feeling a spanking – what's the point of that?

There was one time Mr. Defeu and I attended a Victorian night at our local dungeon space. For fun at one point, he bent me over and caned me with all my period clothes on – bustle included! I had to start laughing, because he was using all his strength and I couldn't feel a thing! But that was just *funny* – not real *fun!*

Eve: Last year you did a bit of party hosting in San Francisco. What was the most fun about throwing a party and did you encounter any frustrations?

continued on page 13

When Zille showed up at a Shadow Lane party in this Betty Page dress, we were all intrigued. Who wouldn't want to know more about a woman who channels the 50's so well?

Zille came to Shadow Lane to shoot "His Two Disobedient Wives" and "Starter Wife, Trophy Wife" co-starring her real life English husband and our favorite immigrant Brit, Clare Fonda.

Zille: The most fun thing was walking around the party, and seeing everyone having such a great time, and knowing I had brought it about! It was a most giddy, wonderful feeling!

The frustrations were the same as they would be for anyone having a large function: people promise things and don't deliver – leaving you to resolve the problem at the last moment; or there are problems with your event space; or people start trying to squabble about some detail of your party that was a compromise you *already* had to make, and it turns into stupid drama that gets in the way of everyone having fun.

But it was really worth all of the frustrations to have that moment, around midnight or so, when I realized that the party had been a total success, and I could just hear thwacks and cries of happy pain, and laughter and happy chatter from all directions.

I want to do another party, but life keeps tossing unavoidable curveballs at me! Someday, in the not too distant future, I hope!

Eve: Is there anything you are working on that we should know about?

Zille: I wish there was because now would be a perfect moment to share it! But I'm not making a living off of modelling anymore, so I just do the occasional shoot for the sheer pleasure of it. If you want to find what I've been doing, you can go to my blog: **http://www.zilledefeu.com**. There are some shoots of me that will be going up on Northern Spanking soon. And I really hope to work with Shadow Lane again! Other than that, I have a story published in *The Spanking Collection: a charity anthology* which I'm very pleased with, and all proceeds of that book go to cancer research charities! I hope 2015 will bring me time for lots more spanking adventures, and if so, I'll come back and tell you about them!

In "Heaven's Waiting Room" Zille plays an intake angel whose duty it is to cleanse naughty souls of their troubling misdeeds before admitting them to paradise. Adorable Maggie Mayhem plays the spirit of a brat who argues that this spanking is too hard for the small sins of which she has been guilty. Naturally, heaven can wait until the full measure of righteous discipline has been dispensed.

In our first spanking survey of the 21st Century, we asked men in the scene: "What's one thing a new spanking playmate could do to charm you?" They replied to this question as follows:

What Charms Men into Spanking?

"Ask for a spanking when she wants one."

"Bend over in front of me, looking over her shoulder with seductive eyes!"

"Honestly discuss her preferences, fantasies and limits emphasizing trust and discretion."

"Either accept her punishment or take control over punishing me."

"Be very cheeky and forthright."

"Offer to do turn-about."

"Let me slap her behind in unexpected, un-planned situations."

"Be intelligent and demonstrate a depth of personality that extends beyond spanking."

"Go top once in a while."

"Wear the right clothes & have a great ass & legs to put in them. She could also ask sheepishly."

"Ask if we can slip under the covers for a short post-spanking nap with her cuddled in my arms. This gets me every time. Also, treat me with respect."

"Wear a thong and flash me in it."

"Be bratty without being bitchy."

"I like for the playmate to get caught up in the moment."

"Open up emotionally and be-come vulnerable. Make me say "Awww... little sweetie, it's okay." I like to comfort and protect them, but hold them accountable and make them re-member when they

haven't done well."

"Offer to switch."

"Dress provocatively."

"Well, just making me happy...allowing me to spank her..."

"Say she was bad and wants to be spanked for what she did."

"I love a good pout."

"Coy smiles are always nice."

"Tell me, out of the blue, that she has been naughty, and needs to be put over my knee."

"Play the misbehaving submissive."

"Be nice, intelligent, willing to accept her chastisement with an open mind/heart, very hygienic, and never tardy!"

"Greet me out of the shower. I hate drying off. I'd like her to dry me off and spank me with a brush."

"Smile."

"Display a sense of humor."

"Wear boy shorts."

"Wear the right clothes."

"Purposely do something that she knows will get her spanked."

"Just be a nice person."

"I like when endearing terms are used towards me; love, sweetie, daddy, darling...although "sir" is not neccessary and I have never required the term even though some submissives have repeatedly called me sir. It is uncomfortable for me to hear. Two other things that have endeared a young lady to me in the past are 1) pouting and 2) when they have said/done something bratty; that instinctive hand motion some girls do to protect their bottom from the potential swat that could be coming is just cute as hell."

"Simply let me know that she would like to put me across her knee."

"No idea; I leave that to her, but getting a slipper out of the wardrobe and holding it suggestively might work."

"Assure me she is trustworthy."

"Climb over my lap without being asked."

"Ask for a spanking."

"Play the roll as I outline it."

"Just show interest in spanking."

"Be honest, up front if it's not going to work, and draw initial guidelines. Limits are a must with a new playmate."

"Be honest and open about themselves, what they want and what they have done – scene-wise or otherwise."

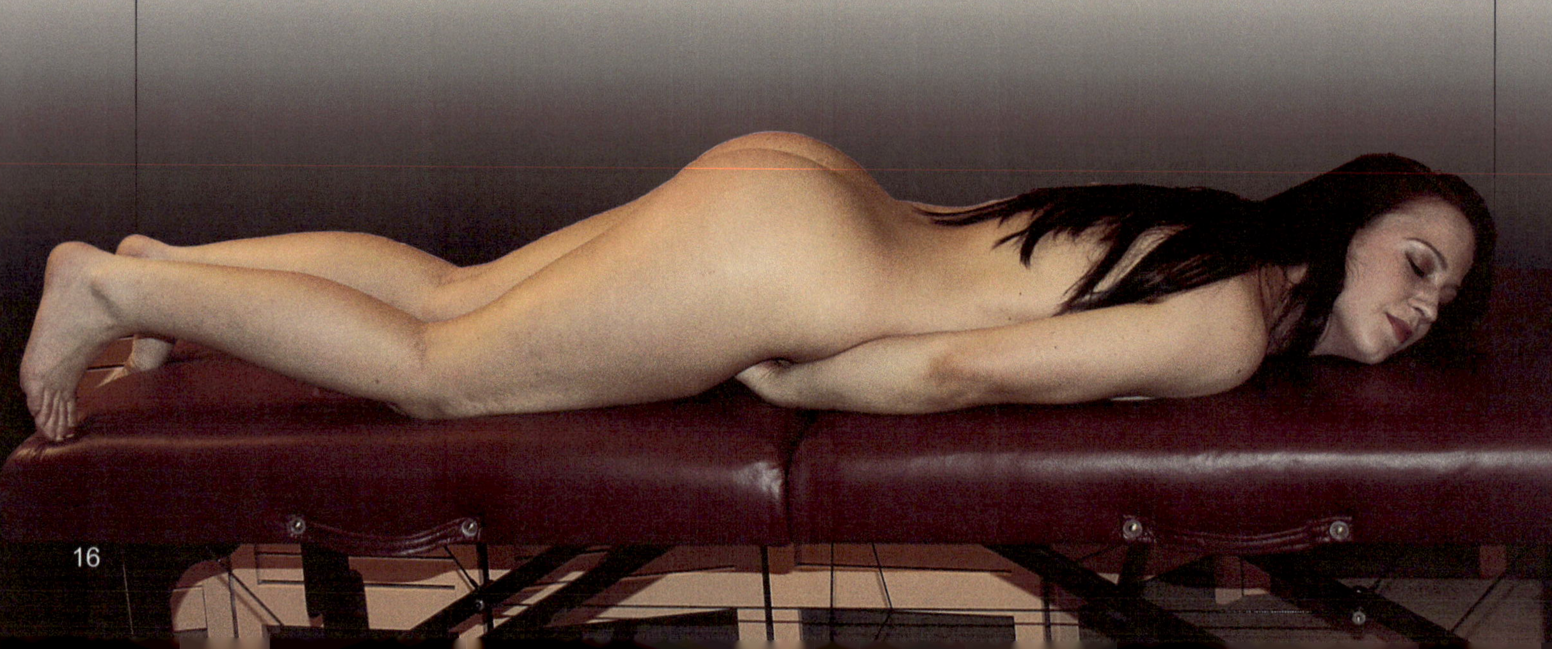

In response to our first spanking survey of the 21st Century, our female readers replied to the question, "What's the one thing a new playmate could do to impress you?" as follows:

What Impresses Women into Spanking?

"Want to spank me."

"Scold me."

"Understand I can say no."

"Start out slow, just don't go right to the bare."

"Mild scolding and "that" look!"

"Communicate and not uber-dom/me."

"Initiate conversation about consent, desires, and limits right off the bat."

"Talk to me and get to know me. Don't just jump in on, are you a sub?!!? Let's PLAY."

"Check with my level of comfort/discomfort."

"Kindness. Consider my needs and desires not just his."

"Be smart. Know the reason behind the play is mental stimulation. The brain moves the body."

"Be respectful."

"Doesn't decide I'm topping from the bottom just because

I'm expressing a preference."

"Sensing how hard he should spank from my body signals and verbal responses."

"Really make an attempt to "get" who I am and play into that."

"Not to stop doing to me what I like!"

"Spend a good amount of time negotiating, and listen well. Then have it show in how he plays."

"Be intelligent & NOT sarcastic."

"Ask me to send them stories that turn me on, and send me the stories, or videos that turn them on."

"Look me in the eyes - ask questions about me - and make me feel like I'm the person they want to get to know."

"Play before, not after dinner."

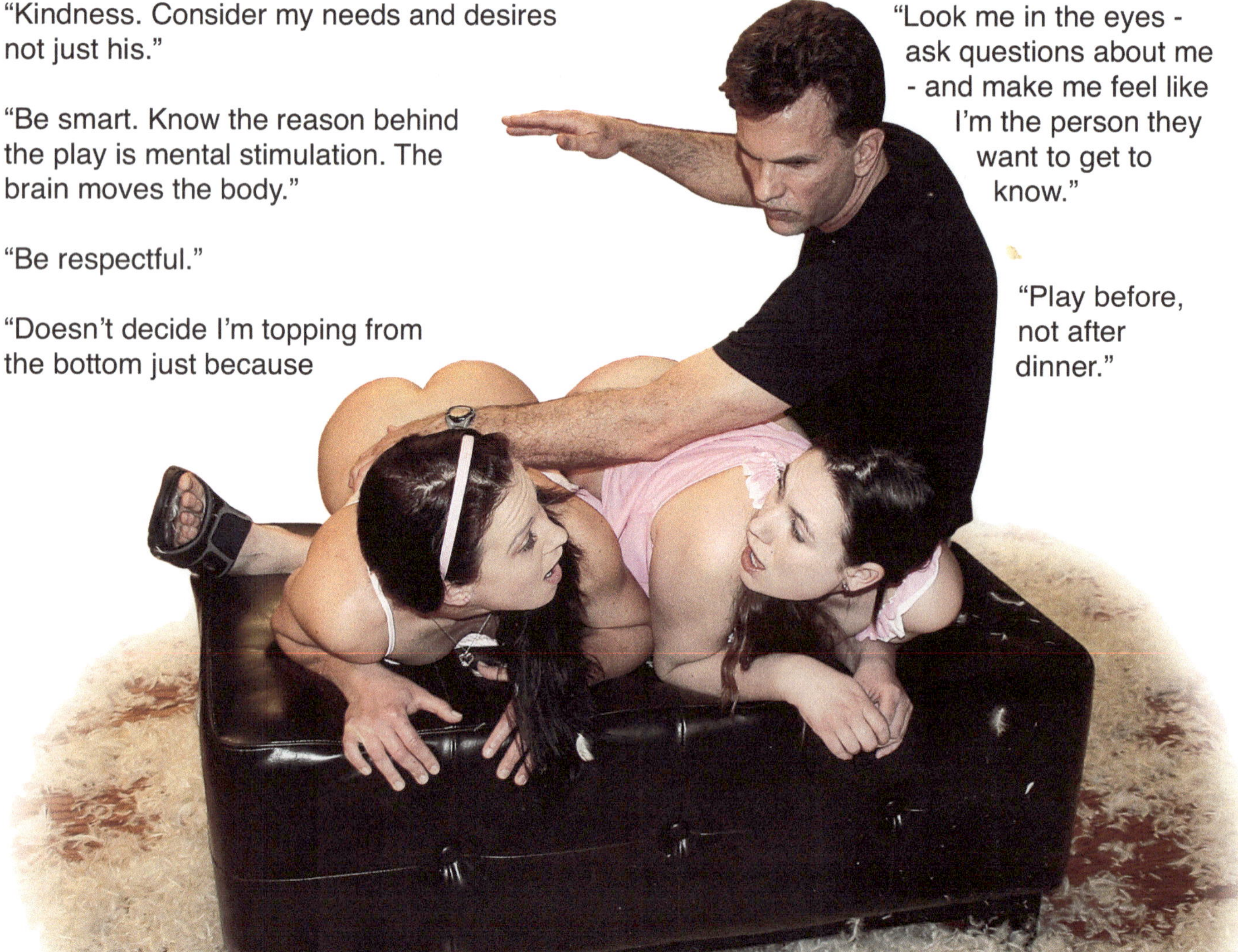

"Talk to me. A lot!"

"Be the stern one."

"Not even ask if I want a spanking. I would love to have a man take me by the arm and spank me."

"Have the ability to give me butterflies."

"NOT show any brutish tendencies."

"They have to be strong and take control over me."

"If he asks about my safeword."

"Give me a nice long warm up."

"Dress nice, be confident."

"Listen to me, and care about what I have to say."

"STAY WITHIN MY LIMITS."

"Talk about more than what he wants to do to me."

"Have amazing weed."

"Not jocularly admire other girls' butts when we're out and expect me to agree."

"Take charge, but in a way that makes me comfortable."

"Ask me what I want to drink."

"Re: digital penetration, he should make it clear he understands that fingers may go from front to back but not back to front. Please guys, spare us this most awkward of teachable moments in real time and just let us know that you're hip to the hygiene before the diddling begins."

"There's something to be said for spontaneity, but sometimes if a guy just lunges, grabs and smacks, it can easily feel like manhandling. Like taking a cookie, you should ask first."

"Doing what he says he's going to do."

"Be a person of substance so that my submission makes sense. Normally I have it way more together than the men I have played with."

"Take his time to spank me so thoroughly that I have to use my safe word. Tears would be cathartic for me."

"Be confident - not arrogant."

"Outthink me."

"Talk about vanilla interests too."

"Don't start too hard or stop too soon. Take time to go through the different layers."

"Smell good."

"Be packing lube and condoms, just in case things get crazy."

"If he's immaculate and flawless, a total metrosexual, he should also have a sense of humor about these things."

"Not expect me to fall to their feet like a slave."

"TALK! One of the things I loved about those early Shadow Lane videos was the wonderful scolding before, during, and after the punishment. There was always a sense of warmth and affection in those videos. Punishment was always for the good of the relationship or misbehavior that could lead to the endangerment of the lady who needed to be taken to task. Great romantic stuff."

The Brat's Pajamas

In response to our readers' many requests that we focus more closely on girls in pajamas, we present a gallery of flannel and cotton clad imps to awaken your coziest midnight spanking fantasies. We begin our tour of Dreamland with the ivory skinned Sybil Hawthorne, one of the most sensitive performers in the scene. Everything about her is natural and charming, from her glamorous hair to her luscious proportions to the glow of submissive fire in her heart. She's as articulate as she is physically expressive and makes a total commitment to emotional release every time she plays.

It isn't a secret that girls into spanking almost always prepare to enjoy their most private and naughtiest fantasies by pulling their pants down, as demonstrated by the beautiful and recently spanked Sybil Hawthorne.

Don't ask a girl you just met to dress for her spanking in pajamas. It's a lot to ask. Pajamas suggest an intimacy and vulnerability that not every lady is willing to expose herself to before complete trust in her top has been established. Yet it is easy to see why this type of outfit is so desirable as garb for a spanking scenario. The culprit is dressed and yet undressed, completely covered, yet instantly exposed with one yank of the pants.

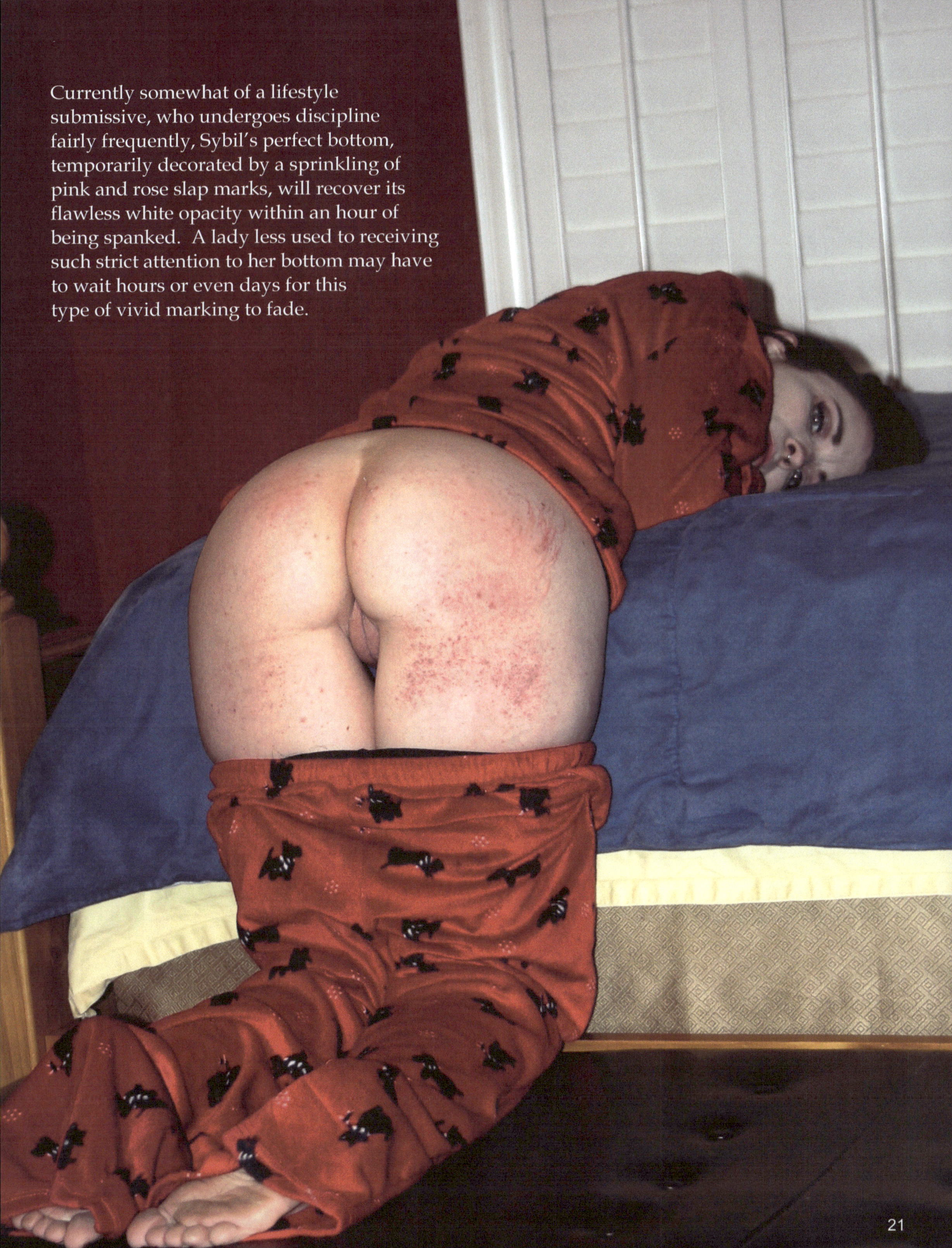
Currently somewhat of a lifestyle
submissive, who undergoes discipline
fairly frequently, Sybil's perfect bottom,
temporarily decorated by a sprinkling of
pink and rose slap marks, will recover its
flawless white opacity within an hour of
being spanked. A lady less used to receiving
such strict attention to her bottom may have
to wait hours or even days for this
type of vivid marking to fade.

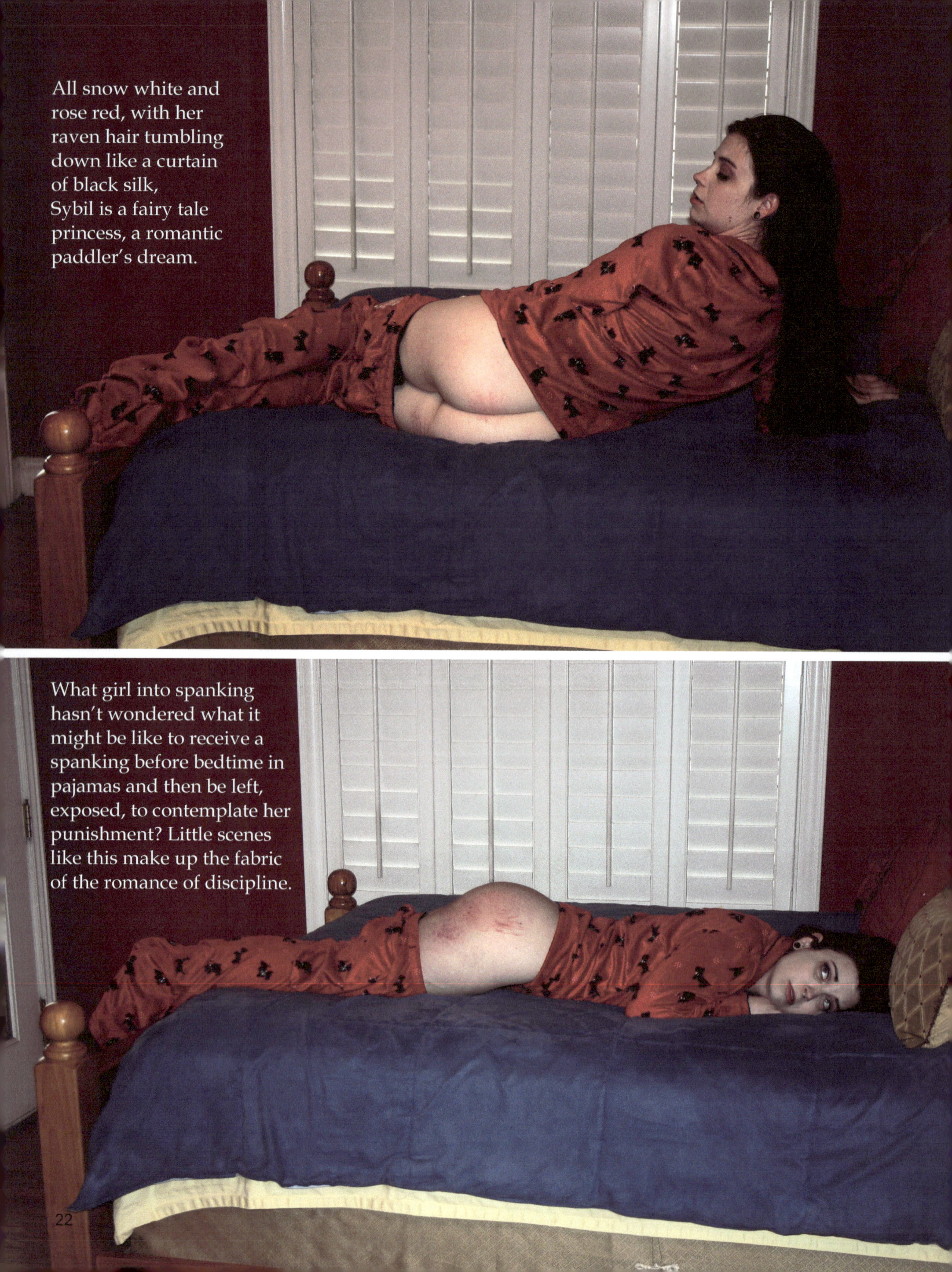

All snow white and
rose red, with her
raven hair tumbling
down like a curtain
of black silk,
Sybil is a fairy tale
princess, a romantic
paddler's dream.

What girl into spanking
hasn't wondered what it
might be like to receive a
spanking before bedtime in
pajamas and then be left,
exposed, to contemplate her
punishment? Little scenes
like this make up the fabric
of the romance of discipline.

Petite, fair skinned, natural redhead Madison Young, looks especially delectable in cotton pajamas. Due to her light complexion, Madison tends to color quickly and deeply from even a hand spanking, but like Sybil, her color tends to fade within thirty to sixty minutes. To reduce marking after a vigorous spanking (if that is your desire, some people cherish these emblems of punishment) apply an ice pack to the spanked area for a few minutes.

Lovely Madison Young suggests even more reasons to love girls in pajamas. Doesn't every submissive appear more vulnerable and tender in accessible soft cotton garb? The relaxed informality of sleepwear, the comfort and security it promises as a girl slips off to dreamland, encourages sensuality.

Sophy's Bedtime Spanking

Miss Sylvia is most displeased with her English house guest, Sophy. She's been so irritating that Sylvia's hand has itched to spank the cheeky redhead.

Sylvia begins to think that maybe she has made it too comfortable for her visitor from across the waves. But Sylvia also knows how to make a girl uncomfortable.

"You think you're smart? I'll make you smarter!"

25

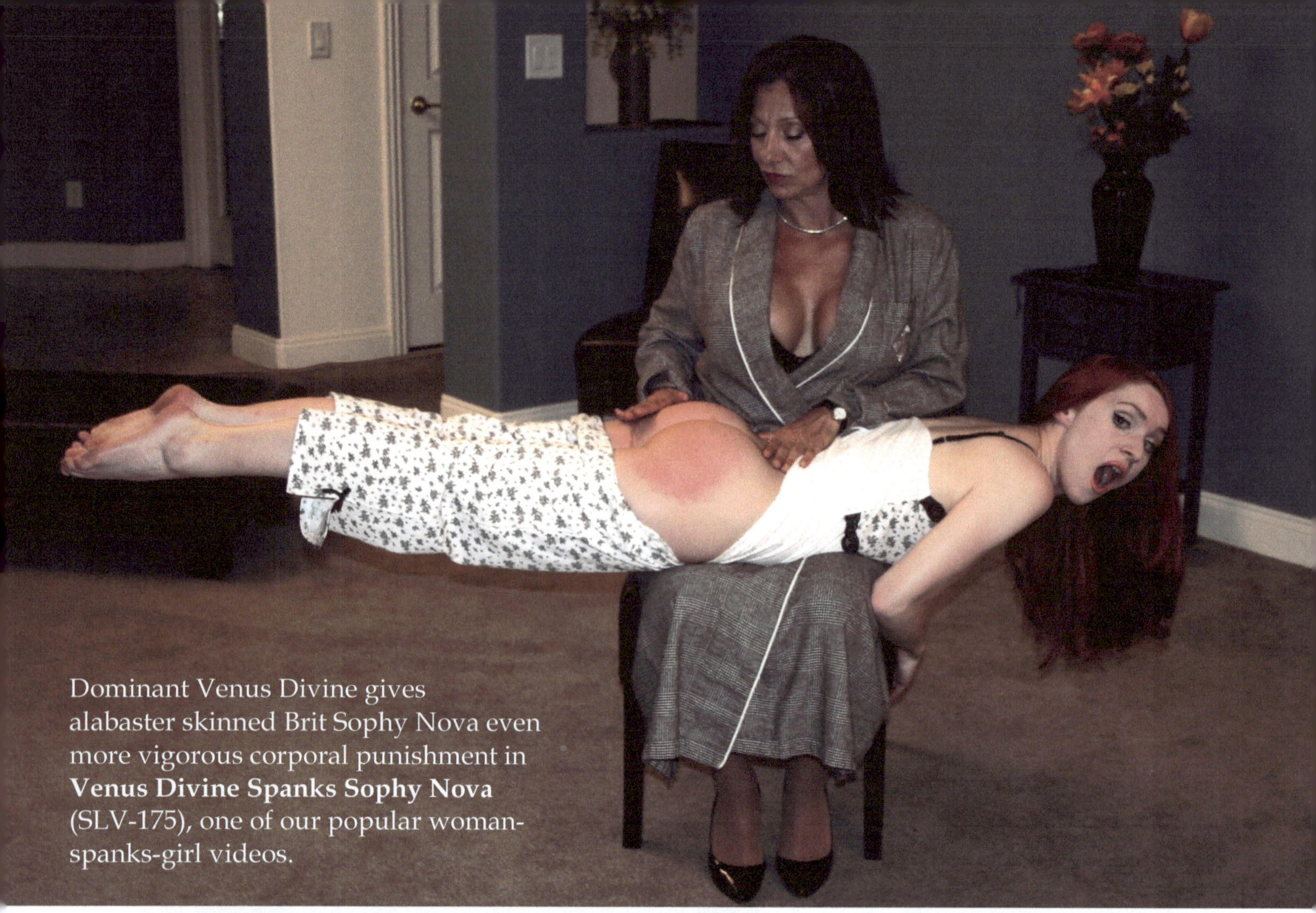

Dominant Venus Divine gives alabaster skinned Brit Sophy Nova even more vigorous corporal punishment in **Venus Divine Spanks Sophy Nova** (SLV-175), one of our popular woman-spanks-girl videos.

Miss Divine lays down the law in a Boston accent that goes well with her confident attitude. Sophy squeals, whimpers and pleads for mercy in a cute English accent. Subbed out UK girls are rocking the 21st century spanking scene.

When a powerful dominant meets a vulnerable submissive and the chemistry between them is correct, a decisive conquest leads to a touching surrender.

Lovely Lena Ramone discusses the pajama girl mystique in the Shadow Lane video, "Playing By Myself" Volume Two, (SLV-165). This series that was created for those who prefer instructional erotica, where the lady speaks directly to them about corporal punishment, while demonstrating self-spanking and also self-pleasuring techniques.

Here Lena shows how easy it is to self-administer a stinging spanking with a birch.

"You have to go over my lap."
"Do I *have* to?"
"You lost the bet and agreed to be spanked."

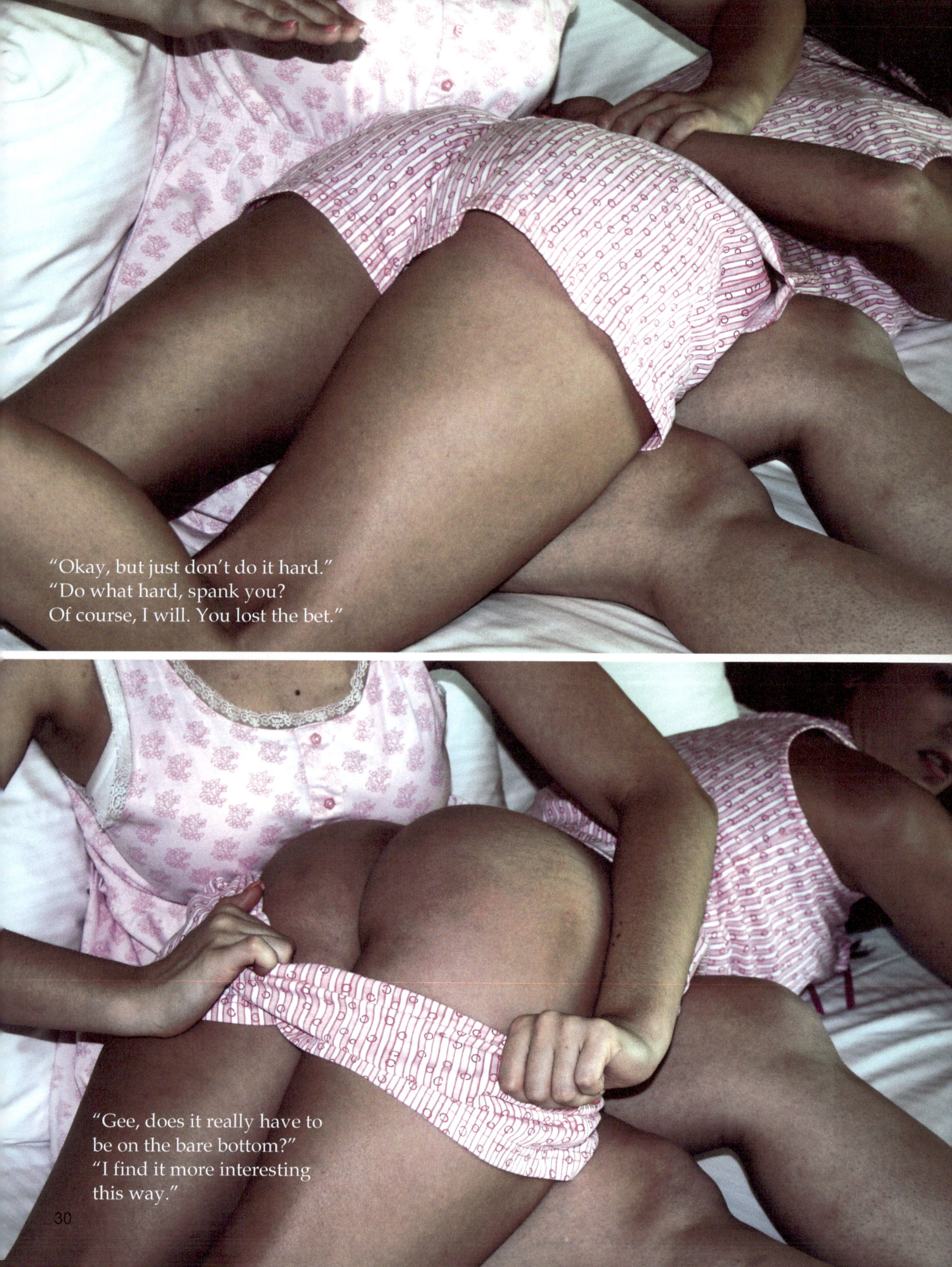

"Okay, but just don't do it hard."
"Do what hard, spank you?
Of course, I will. You lost the bet."

"Gee, does it really have to
be on the bare bottom?"
"I find it more interesting
this way."

"This will teach you not to bet against me when I am playing Broadway show tune bar trivia. You lost our money and we had to buy our own drinks! But at least I can enjoy this!"

"Mmmmm, I'm feeling sleepy, and horny. But I don't see what you could possibly enjoy about doing this."

"I'll wake you up!"

"That was enough of a warm up.
Get ready for real spanking you
have coming now!"

"I like the sounds you're making now,
those yelps and whimpers. They show
I'm getting through to you."

"You're so bad, I'm sure
you're getting wet!
I think I'll inspect you."

Great Expectations – The Missing Chapter

by Philip Kemp

[Has there ever, in all English literature, been a female more sorely in need of a good spanking than young Estella in Great Expectations*? Spoilt, snobbish, conceited, presuming upon her beauty as licence to insult anyone she considers her social inferior, this insufferable teenage miss is surely a prime candidate for a good long thorough bottom-warming.*

Well, it seems that Charles Dickens may have secretly agreed. Tireless as ever, the researchers of the Camden Institute for Disciplinary Studies have unearthed, stuffed down the back of a sofa at Gad's Hill Place, several yellowed pages covered with The Inimitable's unruly scrawl. The episode, it appears, would have fitted into Chapter 19 of Great Expectations *as we have it today, just after Pip has come to take his leave of Miss Havisham before departing for London.*

Did Dickens ever intend this episode to form part of the novel as published? Probably not. He had a shrewd grasp of what his public expected of him, and must have been well aware that a scene such as this would have offended conventional Victorian tastes. More than likely, he wrote it for his own satisfaction, and perhaps for the amusement of a few close friends. Thanks to this serendipitous find, we can now all share in that amusement – and satisfaction.]

Sarah Pocket conducted me down, as if I were a ghost that must be seen out. She could not get over my appearance, and was in the last degree confounded. I said "Good-bye, Miss Pocket," but she merely stared, and did not seem collected enough to know that I had spoken.

I was making my way through the garden, reflecting on all that had befallen since I first ventured there as a lad, when a voice behind me made me startle.

"You again, boy? It seems you cannot keep away from this house!"

I turned in amazement. Estella stood there, the familiar scornful smile on her face.

"Miss Estella!" I stammered. "I – I thought you were away!"

"You – you thought that, did you?" she retorted mockingly. "And why might you think so, boy?"

"Why, Miss Havisham said you were abroad, educating for a lady."

"And so I was, and soon shall be again. But abroad is not a prison, you know. One may travel to and from it as one wishes. As for 'educating for a lady' – was I not lady enough before?"

Her question left me in confusion. "I – I couldn't say, miss."

"You – you couldn't say," she mocked me again. "Why, of course you couldn't say. What would an ignorant little wretch like you know of ladies? Although" – and here she commenced circling round and round me, derisively pulling at the flaps and lapels of my garments, for all the world as though I were a hen to be plucked – "no doubt you now think yourself quite the gentleman, in all your finery? *Mister* Pip; is that how I must call you now, boy?"

"No, Miss Estella."

"'No, Miss Estella. No, indeed. A crow in borrowed feathers is a crow still, and you in your new-bought garb are no less the little coarse monster that you always were."

I could find no answer to this, but stood mute, inwardly stricken but resolved to let no trace of my hurt show in my face. Estella, though, saw through me.

"Do I hurt you, boy? Am I as insulting as ever? And as pretty?"

"Prettier than ever," said I, truthfully enough. "And even more insulting."

"Am I though?" she said, and slapped my face. "Then tell me how you like *that* for an insult."

She had slapped me once before, I recalled, and then I had taken it meekly enough, as if slapping me were no more than her right. But I was older now, and my recent good fortune had given me some inklings of self-regard. I felt an unaccustomed sentiment stirring within me, more akin to anger than resentment.

"You had no call to do that, Miss Estella," said I.

TARSIS

She gazed at me in unfeigned surprise. To her, I conceived, it was as if a fly that she had swatted should raise its buzzy voice against her in reproach.

"No call, boy? Why, you little wretch, do you think I need call? I shall slap you if I wish, and as often as I wish."

She made as if to do so again, but I stepped back and, rather to my own amazement, found myself saying, "Miss Estella, I should strongly advise you not to do that again."

Astonishment was now mixed with fury in her expression. "You *advise* me? You, a coarse, common labouring-boy, advise *me*?" She laughed contemptuously. "Why, boy, I do believe that this great fortune you have come into has turned your brain; or what little of it you ever had. You have become an even greater fool than that poor stumbling booby of a blacksmith who raised you." She laughed again; an ugly sound it seemed to me, for all her prettiness. "Foolishness, perhaps, is catching."

For an instant her words took me aback, for I had no reason to think she had ever heard of Joe, still less that she knew anything of him. But this feeling was soon overtaken by a sense of indignation; not on my own account, but that of poor goodhearted Joe, who assuredly had never done the least thing to offend her. "Estella," said I, "you should not speak of Joe in those terms; it's not right."

Only after the words had left my mouth did I realise that, for the first time, I had taken the liberty of addressing Estella by her bare name, unprefaced with 'Miss'. It may have been this, as much as my reproof, that aroused her ire. At all events she exclaimed, "What? Again? You common wretch!" and, stepping swiftly forwards, slapped me once more; this time with all her force.

Had I taken but a moment for reflection, I should never have done what I then did. It was illconsidered; it was imprudent; it was even, you might say, in the last degree unchivalrous. But in the burning flash of that slap, which fairly made my teeth rattle, it was as if Estella appeared to me in a new and diminished light; no longer as a selfpossessed and remarkably pretty young lady, as

far above me in status and accomplishments as she was in personal beauty, but as a spoilt, malicious child, delighting in her own cruelty. And it was as a spoilt child that I took it upon myself to treat her.

There was nearby us a wooden garden seat, ancient but sturdy. Seizing her wrist – for she seemed disposed to slap me yet again – I pulled her over to the seat and sat down upon it. So astonished was she at this turn of events, she scarce resisted me, but gaped at me in wide-eyed disbelief. "What…? How dare you!" she gasped. "Unhand me this instant, you clod-hopping boor!"

"All in good time," said I, as I drew her face-down over my lap. "First, Estella, you have a lesson to learn here today. You may be educated for a lady; all well and good, I'm sure. But did none of your educators ever tell you that you cannot abuse, and insult, and assault any person as the whim takes you – or at least, not without risk of consequence?"

She struggled furiously, calling me every injurious name she could light upon and threatening me with the most bloodthirsty retributions; but I had her pinned fast, and her struggles were in vain. One part of me – the old Pip, as it were – stood by aghast, trembling that I should venture such temerity. But this new, bolder Pip who had now asserted himself seemed resolved to exact retribution, come what might.

She wore a dress of full, gathered, rose-pink satin that would surely have impeded any design of serious chastisement. But having proceeded so far, and having committed to such a rash course of action, I felt I owed it to myself – and to Joe, and to whomsoever else had felt the lash of her contempt – to carry it through to some worthwhile effect. Accordingly I grasped her dress by the hem, and together with her petticoats turned it up well above her slim waist. This action brought a fresh volley of outraged invective from Estella, but also had the advantage – at least, from my point of view – of hampering her attempts to place a protective hand over the predestined target area.

Which area, it could scarcely be gainsaid, present-ed a most appealing aspect – being pleasingly rounded, and altogether quite ideally shaped for the treatment it was about to receive. A pair of cream-coloured silken drawers, tastefully trimmed with lace, fitted snugly over Estella's posterior curves, and would – I felt sure – provide little if anything by way of protection for those tender mounds.

By now, since she could be in no doubt as to what I intended, Estella's cries of indignation were reaching such a pitch of shrillness that I felt sure someone would come rushing to her aid. But no-body came. Miss Havisham, of course, could not descend the stairs from her rooms on the first sto-rey; but Sarah Pocket must surely be well within earshot. Yet if so, it seemed she felt no inclination to act the protector. She too, after all, had felt the sharp edge of Estella's tongue now and again; and might it not be she concurred with me, that the young lady's pride and wilfulness richly deserved the reward I was about to bestow?

At all events, pending the arrival of some gallant knight bent on rescuing the damsel, I – or rather, this new, resolute Pip – was intent on requiting Estella for her arrogance.

"You have slapped me, Estella," said I, resting my hand on that aspect of her anatomy most sweetly shaped for punitive attentions; "you have abused me, and insulted me, and treated me with con-tempt, all with no good cause - other than that it amused you to do so. What I am about to do, then, will be done with *very* good cause; but I think it will also amuse me, and I mean to do it well."

So saying, I raised my hand, and brought it down with no little vigour. The yelp thus elicited – equally compounded, it seemed to me, of surprise, pain and outrage – was satisfyingly shrill, and re-assured me that my first essay in the chastisement of young ladies was well gauged. I therefore pro-ceeded in the same style, spanking Estella hard and steadily, and taking care that my strokes were evenly distributed across the full expanse of her soft and squirming hinderparts.

Had anyone suggested to me, not three minutes earlier, that I would ever dare lay peremptory hands upon Estella – and more than that, that I would have the audacity to administer upon her person condign punishment of the kind normally reserved for wayward schoolchildren – I should certainly have regarded that person as ripe for the madhouse. Yet here I was, most indubitably doing it – and doing it, what was more, with a degree of determination of which, I am sure, none of my ac-quaintance would ever have believed me capable.

Determination and, I must in all honesty confess, enjoyment. Had I not, over the years since first we met, built up a substantial debit of unearned con-tempt, abuse, disdain and downright scorn on her account? – all which heavy obligation I was now able to discharge to my ready gratification. For not only was the young lady being subjected – as her vocal reactions amply testified – to a fair de-gree of discomfort, but her pride, on which I knew she set great store, was now humbled as perhaps never before in her life. Very few young women, I imagine, could retain much in the way of dignity while being upended and soundly spanked – and Estella, on her current showing, was surely not among them.

"Ow! Aah! Stop it this instant!" she shrieked. "How dare you? Let me – oww! – go at once! You brute! I'll have you thrown in jail – flogged – exe-cuted! Aahh! Oww! Oh it hurts!"

This last observation was, I felt sure, no more than the truth. The palm of my hand was starting to sting a good deal; how much more acutely, I re-flected, must that sting be felt by the tender flesh upon which my palm was now repeatedly de-scending. I well remembered the effect of Tickler, so often wielded by my sister in her righteous in-dignation. My hand was no Tickler; but then Es-tella, I surmised, was far less inured to physical chastisement than I.

At all events, I was resolved to make an impres-sion upon her she should not soon forget; and to that end I continued to spank her roundly, despite her threats and protests. Already a roseate hue was making itself visible through the close-fitting cream silk of her drawers, attesting to the warmth I was kindling beneath them. I was sorely tempted to lower the garment and view the full effects of my handiwork, but reflected that the humiliation to her modesty might be too great for her to en-dure.

In all my dealings with Estella I had known her scornful, contemptuous, mocking, haughty and (at best) indifferent; but I had never yet seen her remorseful, nor ever for a moment imagined that I should. Yet bit by bit, as her spanking proceeded, her tone changed; where she had waxed indignant, she implored; where she had issued threats, she now uttered pleas. And in due course there came from her lips the one word I never thought to hear from her; and that word was "Sorry."

With it there came a flood of tears. Not tears of fury, but tears of helpless penitence, in racking sobs that touched my heart. I ceased spanking her and stroked the punished mounds; they felt fiery hot to the touch, confirming to me that my retribution had been as effective as I could wish.

I re-ordered Estella's clothing and lifted her up. She clung to me, sobbing. Broken phrases reached my ears, in which I could make out the words "forgive," "please," "better" and once again "sorry." I held her and thought I had never heard sweeter sounds.

After a time she lifted her tear-stained face to mine. Once before, after I had fought with the pale young gentleman, she had let me kiss her cheek. I had thought then that the kiss was carelessly granted and worth little. But now it was she who kissed me, and I felt that it was worth a great deal. Not least since the kiss was accompanied by a whispered "Thank you."

With those words she rose, and vanished into the house without a single backward glance. I sat a few minutes, wondering greatly – at myself and at her, and at the events of the preceding quarter-hour. I might well have thought I had dreamt them, were it not for a still perceptible stinging sensation in the palm of my right hand. I could not help reflecting with a certain satisfaction that Estella must be experiencing a similar sensation elsewhere about her person; similar, but a good deal more vivid and lasting in its effect. Or so I fervently hoped.

In due course I shook myself out of my reverie, rose and gained the gate. Clear of the house, I made the best of my way back to Pumblechook's.

Domestic
Disturbance

"I didn't realize I was supposed to really clean the house, Mr. Simms. I thought I was just *playing* the maid."

"Well, you were wrong, Miss Hawthorne. In this recession, no one does just one job anymore."

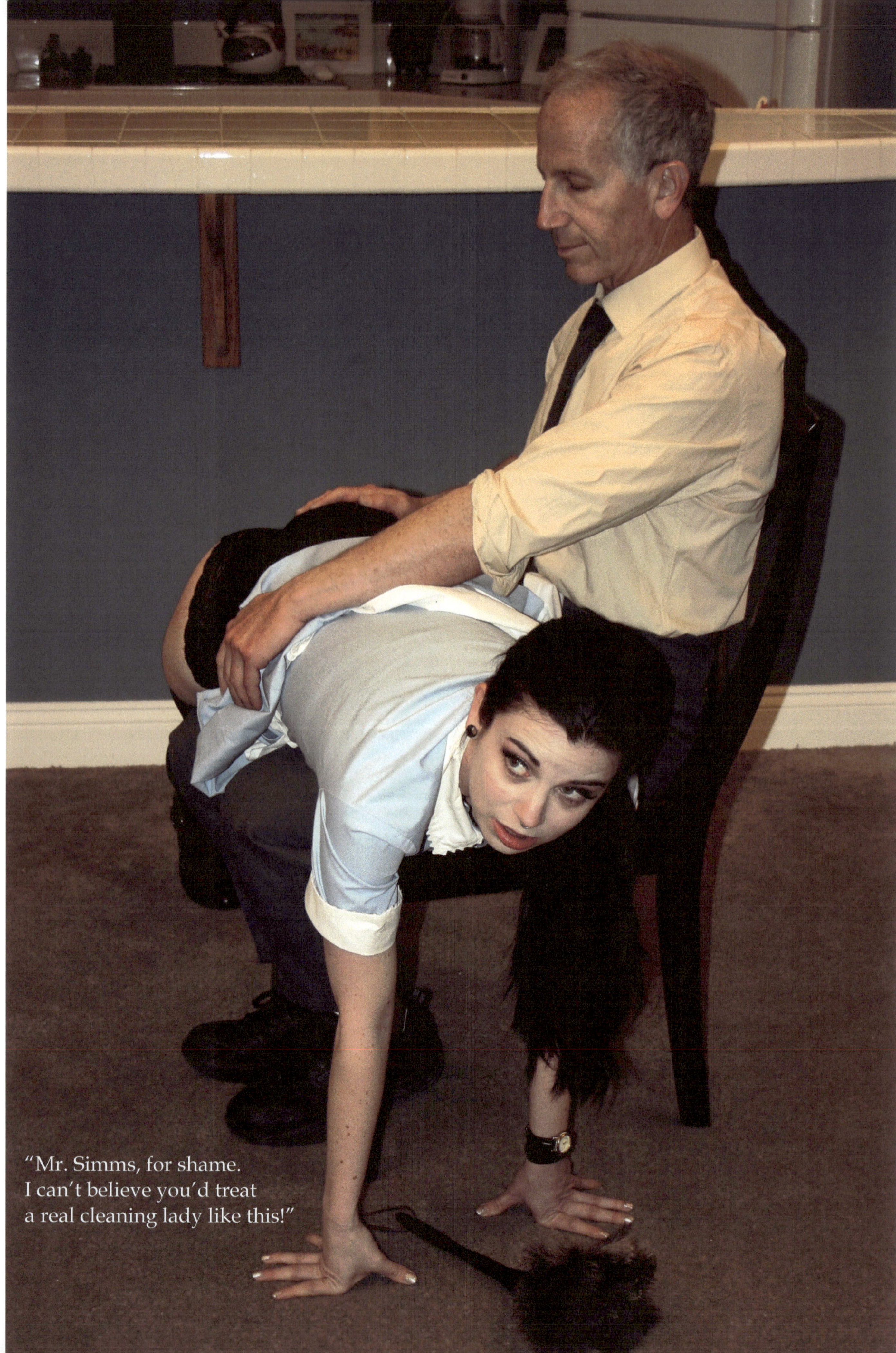

"Mr. Simms, for shame.
I can't believe you'd treat
a real cleaning lady like this!"

"No, because she'd be
doing her job instead
of trying to distract
me with her sexy
black lingerie."

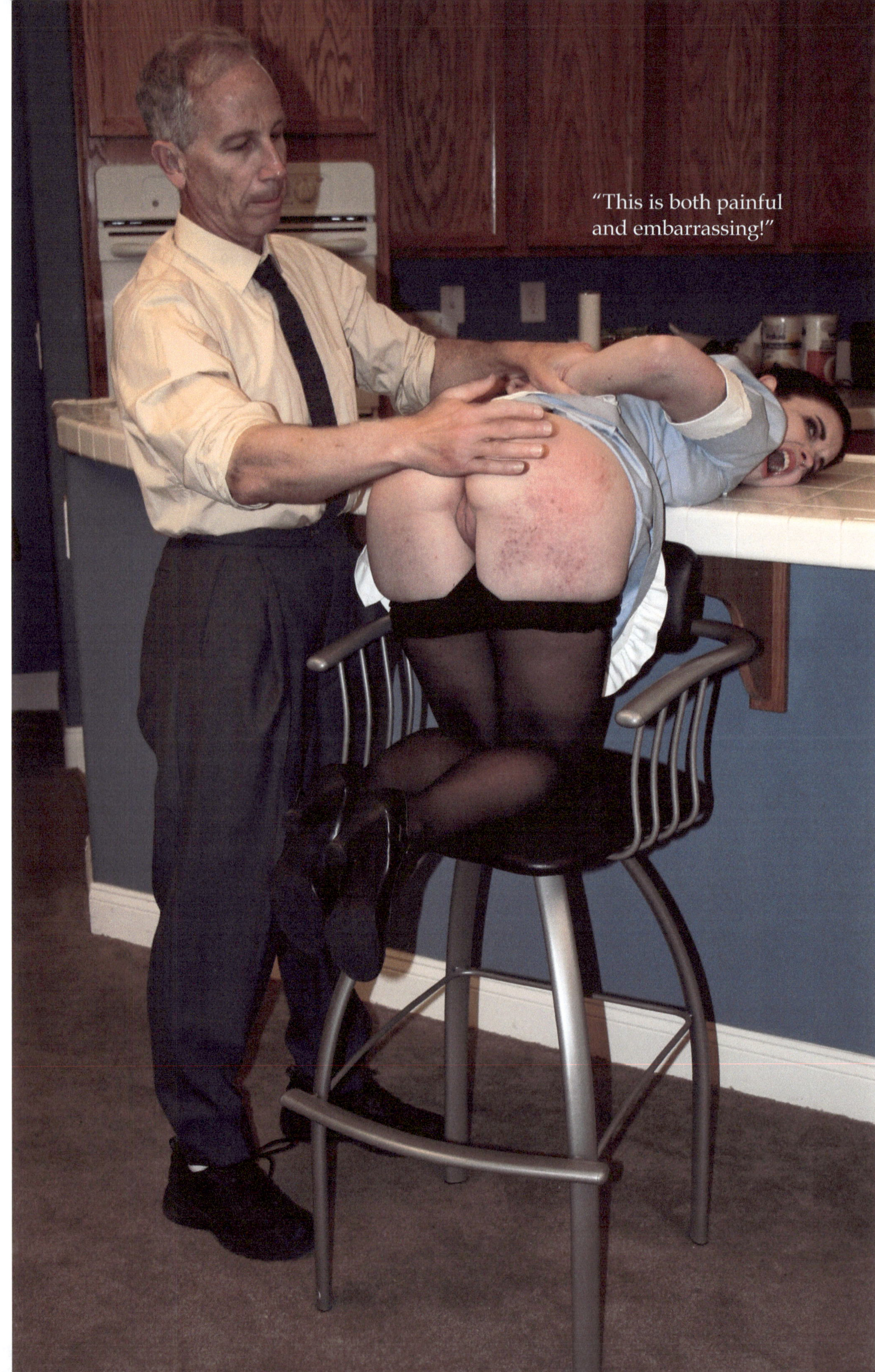

"This is both painful
and embarrassing!"

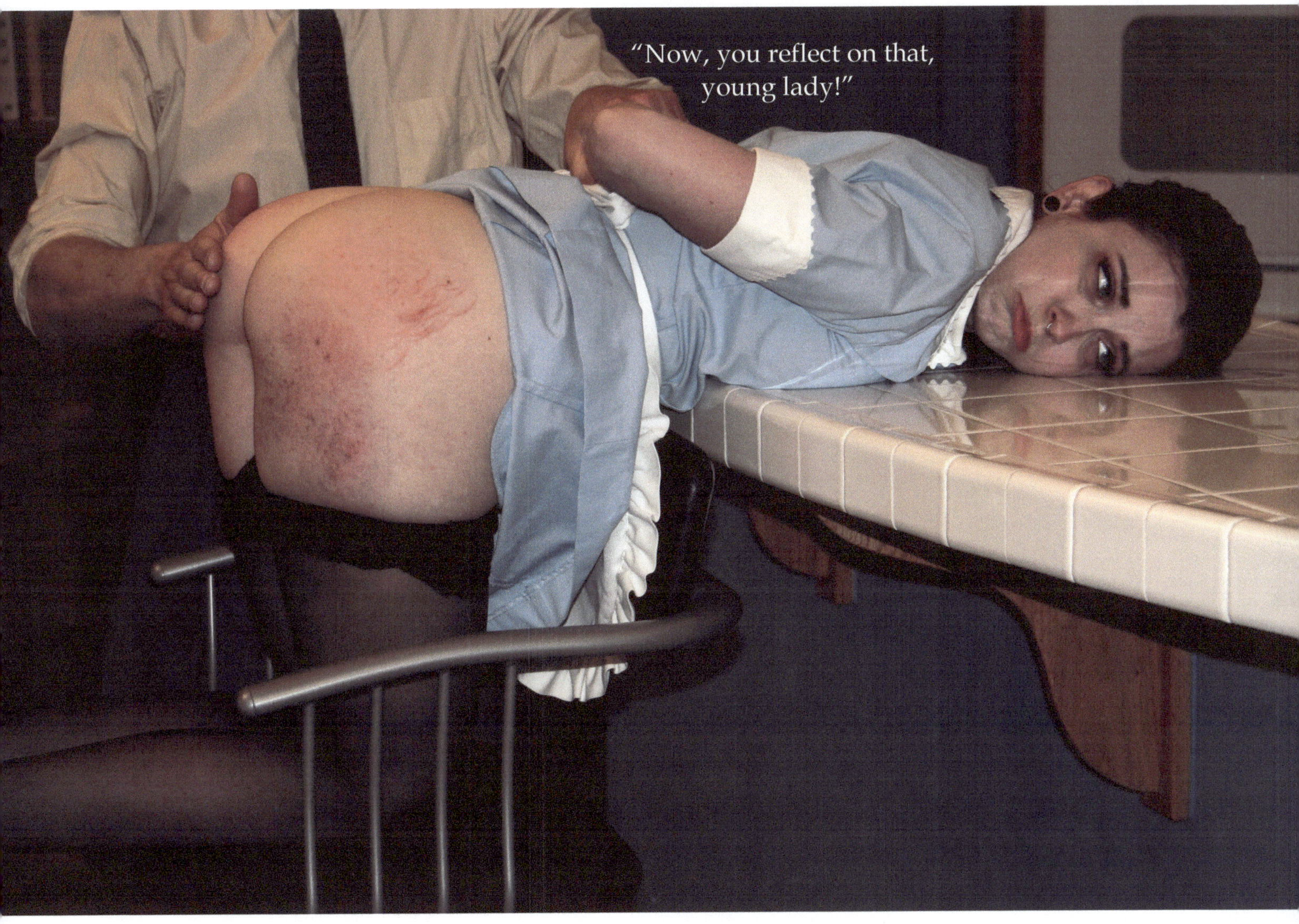
"Now, you reflect on that,
young lady!"

Eve Howard's
Spanking Scrapbook

What with the identical pose
and similar demeanor, doesn't
Sarah Gregory bear an uncanny
resemblance to me, 29 years ago,
just about when she was born?
Gets you thinking.

Emerging from a truly Rip Van Winkelian retirement of almost 20 years, I made my video comeback as a spanker in October of 2011, topping the scrumptious Sybil Hawthorne.

The second part of
my comeback video,
**Eve Howard's
Disciplinary Reviews**,
features the spunky, shapely
Cheyenne Jewell, my local
Vegas go-to girl.
Bursting with energy and animal
spirits, this born and bred farm girl
walks in beauty. When she shows
up for work, bringing her pretty
wardrobe, her shining, healthy,
natural good looks and easy
affability, you can't help but smile.

With that bod that just won't
quit and the best reactions,
she delivers everything the
connoisseur looks for in
a spankee.

I spanked Madison Young in the opening scene **of Paddled, Pleasured and Purged**, preparing her for a subsequent session with a behavior modification expert at our discipline therapy clinic. Madison was only one year out from having her first baby when this video was filmed and she had already gotten her slim, curvy figure back. This made her exactly the right size to fit across my lap. Star of some of our most popular (explicitly sexual) videos, Madison is a dedicated sex educator, adult producer and erotic performance artist. Her artistry is never lost on a spanking audience, nor is her natural peachy-creamy-strawberry blonde charms.

My friend Clare Fonda (whose alter-ego Jamie Foster does such scandalous things on clips4sale) was the person who convinced me that it was time to get back in front of the camera. On the 4th of July we co-starred in a series of short vignettes shot for our respective download sites.

This breast-spanking scene, in which Clare bullied me severely for some imagined slight, had me screaming for mercy in mere minutes. It was a fan favorite on clips4sale for many weeks.

In this clip, Clare plays a lapsed Lambda Sigma Zeta girl and I play the senior sister sent to administer discipline to her for disgracing the sorority. This is an oft-repeated theme in our **Our Sorority** video series. In this case her punishment consisted of me tickling her, slapping her breasts and finally, forcing her to suck on a bar of soap while being tickled some more.

I like the way Clare's cute cougar body looks in this scene. And of course the way she let me abuse her. I honestly never knew I had it in me. This vignette length clip is affixed to the end of our video, "Venus Divine Spanks Sophy Nova" (SLV-175).

Paris Kennedy, shown here on her knees to Clare Fonda, got us invited to an exclusive models' party, hosted by Girdlebound.com, the largest purveyor of vintage and retro style foundations on the internet. Girdlebound's generous founder gifted us with numerous delightful undergarments, including classic open bottom girdles, stockings, garter belts and bras. All of these will be appearing in future Shadow Lane videos. Thanks, Girdlebound!

We managed to get at least one shot where Clare wasn't holding a glass of wine. These sheer, open bottom, slip girdles are flattering and sexy. Wearing one on a first spanking date without panties on underneath is guaranteed to intrigue and ignite any top guy with a retro bent.

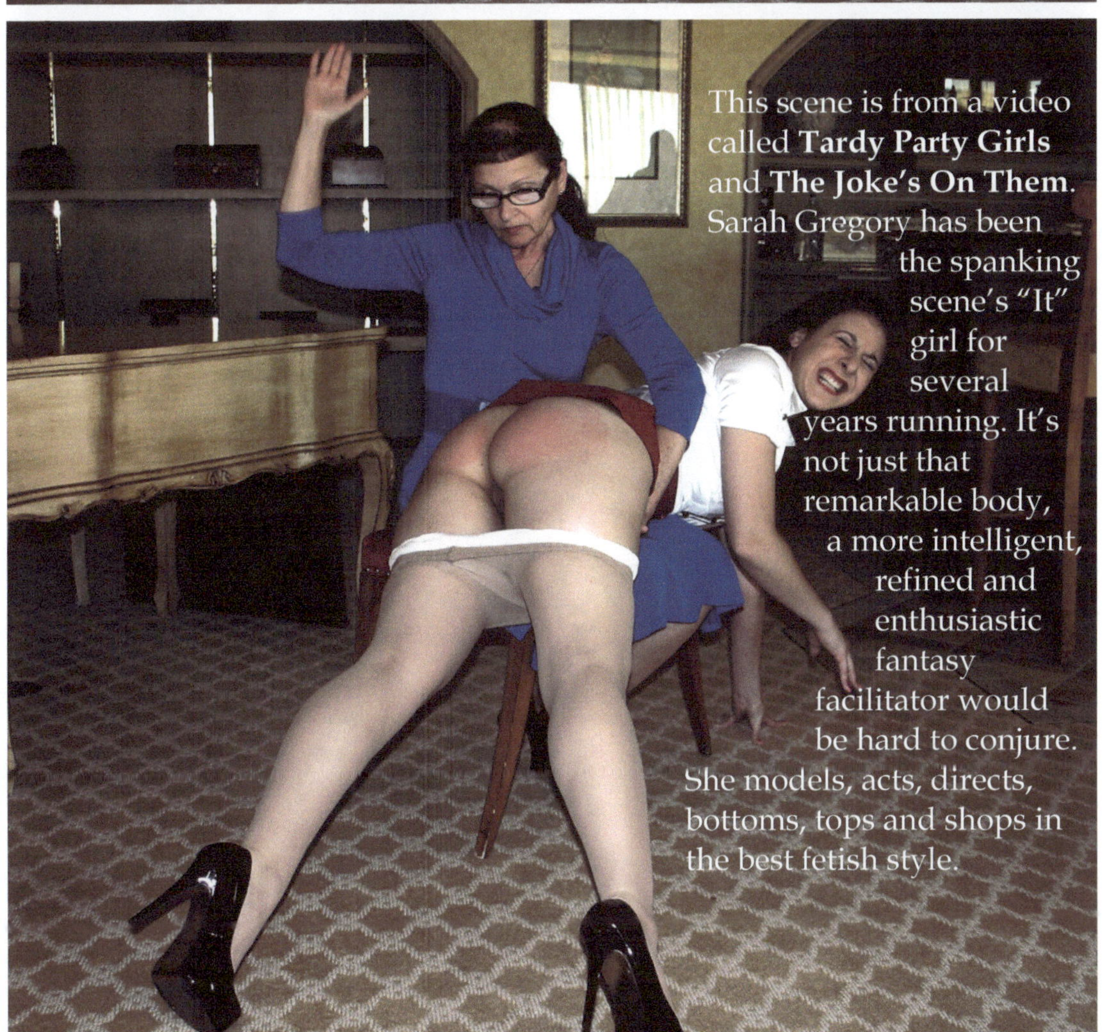

Two of my favorite shots of me spanking Sarah Gregory during the 2013 Shadow Lane Labor Day party weekend in Las Vegas.

This scene is from a video called **Tardy Party Girls** and **The Joke's On Them**. Sarah Gregory has been the spanking scene's "It" girl for several years running. It's not just that remarkable body, a more intelligent, refined and enthusiastic fantasy facilitator would be hard to conjure. She models, acts, directs, bottoms, tops and shops in the best fetish style.

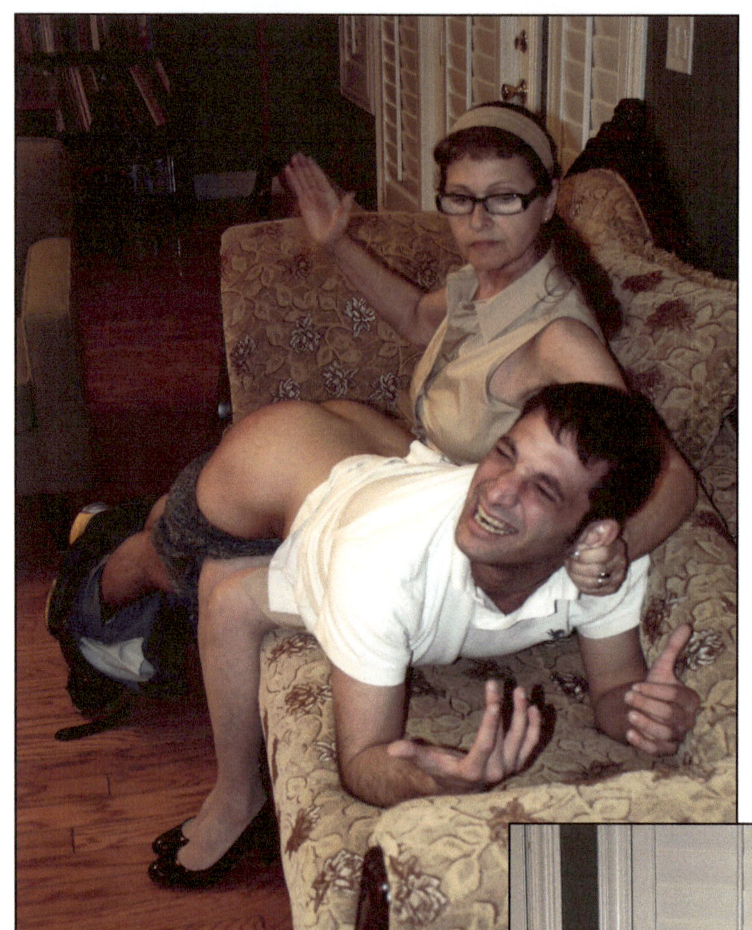

I spanked Kidd Dynamite in my first fem dom video with a male spankee since I went to Nu-West/Leda in the 90's to shoot "David Meets Shadow Lane." My victim is a local who reacted quite immaturely to his discipline, yelling his head off and whining for me to stop before I'd even gotten warmed up. He could barely take my hand, no less a paddle. But that's the way it goes with a model. Every video is like a blind date, you don't know if it's a good match until you're in the midst of it.

Spanking 301

Presenting another episode in our educational spanking series. The opening chapter of Spanking 301 features Nikki Rouge in the top position and Snow Mercy as the spankee. In this segment, the lesson is about how a person who is shorter, smaller or slighter of frame than the person she is topping, can still maintain strict control over his or her submissive. Amazonian Snow Mercy, at 5'10", towers over the willowy, wasp-waisted, 5'8" Nikki Rouge. But Nikki possesses all the switchable skill and brash confidence she needs to discipline her dominant girlfriend to perfection.

Professor Nikki Rouge begins with everyone's favorite, basic open handed spanking on the bare bottom, belaboring the voluptuous backside of her bosom buddy, the beautiful Snow Mercy, until a magenta tinge suffuses the brunette's creamy skin.

Nikki Rouge demonstrates the popular double-handed aim-and-release strapping technique, using a Jem Creations Irish leather strap that has been applied to dozens of Shadow Lane girl bottoms over the past twenty-five years. A good leather strap will last a lifetime.

Another gift sent to Shadow Lane from Ireland years ago was the famous Brat Smacker leather paddle, recommended for ample seats. A large paddle spreads the sting out and produces even coloration when symmetrically laid across bare cheeks.

Here Nikki demonstrates correctly aiming and placing stinging swats with one of our Schoolmaster canes, hand manufactured for us by Keith Jones. No stranger to caning, Snow obediently holds her position for the classic English form of corporal punishment.

Curvy Girls

The spanking world loves curvy girls. Here are some of our most popular fiercely real models revealing both their voluptuous charms and engaging personalities in scenes from a variety of Shadow Lane videos.

Shannon Rose appeared in only one video before disappearing out of the scene. What a shame! She gave a fantastic performance as the naughty bride of Max Maximovich in our video **A Lover's Quarrel** (SLV-109).

Kristiana Fleur played a lady into spanking who engages aversion therapist Danny Chrighton to help her correct some of her more egregious faults in **Spanking Housecall** (SLV-134). Beguilingly submissive Kristiana is a lifelong spanking enthusiast.

Rucca Page is one of our favorite curvy girls. In **Dangerous Blondes** (SLV-131) she plays a nurse at the Braemar Clinic who is a little too curious about the therapy treatments the patients are receiving not to ask for a demonstration of the clinic's healing and revitalizing techniques. The treatment is administered by Arthur Sire.

Luscious brunette Jewell Marceau is punished and embarrassed by Mistress Gemini for various infractions in **Disciplinarian Librarian** (SLV-128) one of our XXX-tra naughty spanking and masturbation videos. As part of her punishment, Jewell is submitted to a caning while being double penetrated by a pair of vibrating balls.

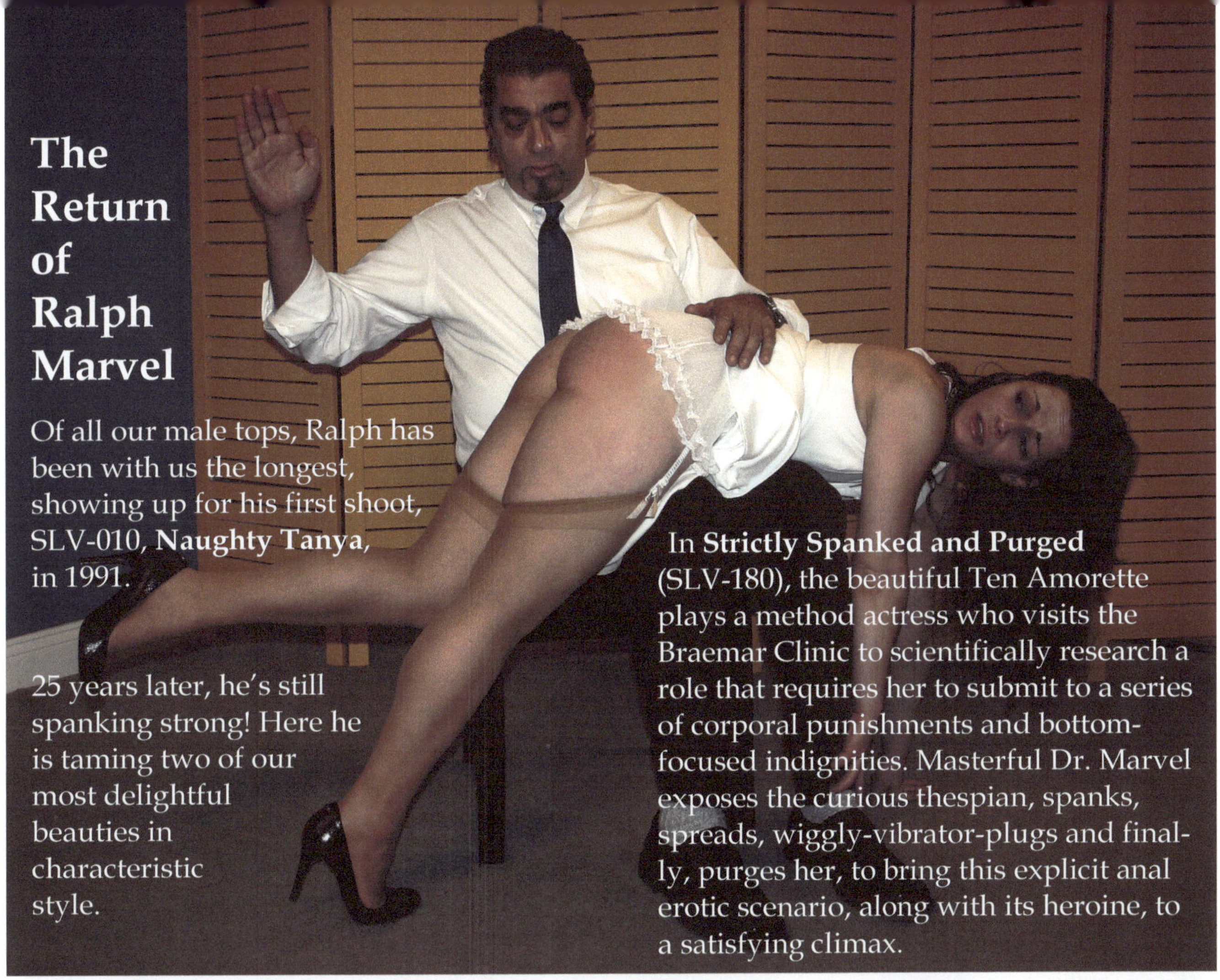

The Return of Ralph Marvel

Of all our male tops, Ralph has been with us the longest, showing up for his first shoot, SLV-010, **Naughty Tanya**, in 1991.

25 years later, he's still spanking strong! Here he is taming two of our most delightful beauties in characteristic style.

In **Strictly Spanked and Purged** (SLV-180), the beautiful Ten Amorette plays a method actress who visits the Braemar Clinic to scientifically research a role that requires her to submit to a series of corporal punishments and bottom-focused indignities. Masterful Dr. Marvel exposes the curious thespian, spanks, spreads, wiggly-vibrator-plugs and finally, purges her, to bring this explicit anal erotic scenario, along with its heroine, to a satisfying climax.

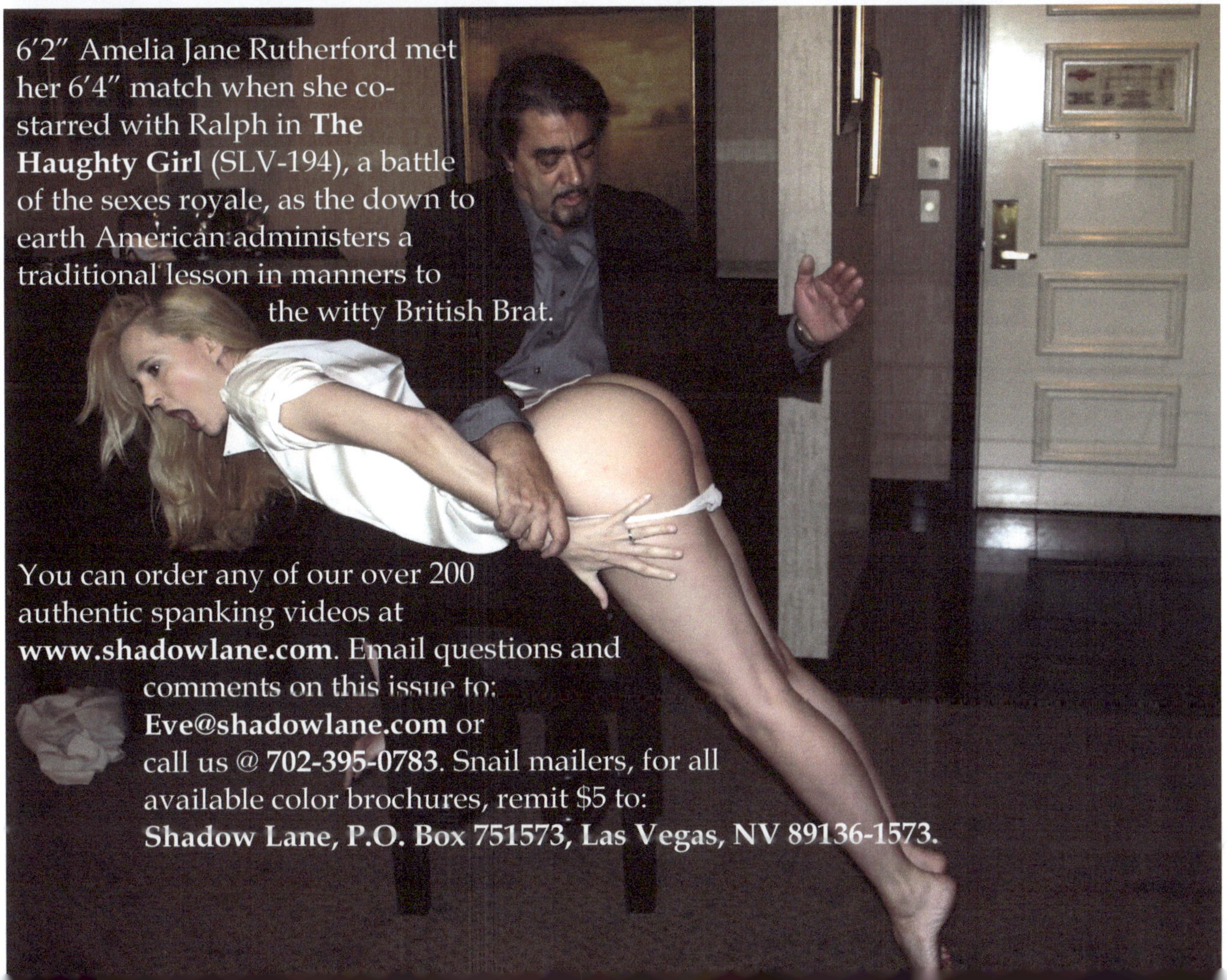

6'2" Amelia Jane Rutherford met her 6'4" match when she co-starred with Ralph in **The Haughty Girl** (SLV-194), a battle of the sexes royale, as the down to earth American administers a traditional lesson in manners to the witty British Brat.

You can order any of our over 200 authentic spanking videos at **www.shadowlane.com**. Email questions and comments on this issue to: **Eve@shadowlane.com** or call us @ **702-395-0783**. Snail mailers, for all available color brochures, remit $5 to: **Shadow Lane, P.O. Box 751573, Las Vegas, NV 89136-1573.**